Escape Underground

KidWitness Tales

KiDWiTNESS
T·A·L·E·S

Escape Underground

CLINT KELLY

BETHANYHOUSE
MINNEAPOLIS, MINNESOTA

6/2002 *Newfound* *5⁰⁰*

Escape Underground, by Clint Kelly
Copyright © 2001 by Focus on the Family
All rights reserved. International copyright secured.

Cover illustration: Chris Ellison
Cover design: Lookout Design Group, Inc.

This story is a work of fiction. With the exception of recognized historical figures, the characters are the product of the author's imagination. Any resemblance to any person, living or dead, is coincidental.

Unless otherwise identified, Scripture quotations are from the HOLY BIBLE, NEW INTERNATIONAL VERSION®. Copyright © 1973, 1978, 1984 by International Bible Society. Used by permission of Zondervan Publishing House. All rights reserved. The "NIV" and "New International Version" trademarks are registered in the United States Patent and Trademark Office by International Bible Society. Use of either trademark requires the permission of International Bible Society.

A Focus on the Family book.
Published by Bethany House Publishers
A Ministry of Bethany Fellowship International
11400 Hampshire Avenue South
Bloomington, Minnesota 55438
www.bethanyhouse.com

Printed in the United States of America by
Bethany Press International, Bloomington, Minnesota 55438

Library of Congress Cataloging-in-Publication Data
Kelly, Clint.
   Escape Underground / by Clint Kelly.
     p. cm. — (KidWitness Tales)
   Summary: In 39 A.D. in Jerusalem, a group of local children must work with the foreign converts they previously tormented when all of their parents are arrested for practicing Christianity.
   ISBN: 1-56179-964-5
   [1. Christian life—History—Early chruch, ca. 30–600—Fiction. 2. Persecution—Fiction. 3. Toleration—Fiction. 4. Jerusalem—History—Fiction.] I. Title. II. Series.
   PZ7.K2932 Es   2001
   [Fic]—dc21   2001003301

1 2 3 4 5 6 7 8 9 10 11 12 13 14 15 / 08 07 06 05 04 03 02 01

To my daughter

Amy

for including everyone

in the fun.

CLINT KELLY loves telling action stories and has published five adventure novels for adults. This is his first adventure for kids. Clint has a particular interest in cryptozoology, the study of mystery animals like Bigfoot and the Loch Ness Monster. Clint used to be a ranger for the U.S. Forest Service. He and his wife, Cheryll, have four children and live in the Pacific Northwest.

CHAPTER 1

Mara made the worst face she could think of. It was unladylike, but so what? You couldn't be a lady 24 hours a day; it was too exhausting.

This meeting of the Way was going nowhere fast. People were arguing and calling each other crazy. They sounded like bees in a hive all buzzing at once. There was nothing of interest to kids here, so why did they have to sit in this stuffy, dreary room?

"You're full of hot desert wind! The world's not going to end!" snapped one.

"You dreamer! Jesus warned of Judgment Day, and it sounded pretty close to me!" said another, pointing an accusing finger.

"That's because you're deaf in both ears and afraid of your own shadow!" the first shot back.

Mara yawned. She dreamed of being in the market by the western temple wall. Admiring the fabrics. Sampling the perfumes. Listening to the clash of languages. Soaking up the crowds and the colors and the excitement. Certainly not sitting here listening to the same old men go on and on about the same old things.

It was time to do something about it!

She arched her eyebrow—a signal to her skinny brother, Nathan. He wrinkled his nose at Obadiah. Obadiah tugged his ear at Sarah. Sarah rubbed both eyes. Mara felt a flush of excitement. The members of the New Israel club were ready. The game was on.

Mara always went first. She stared at a perspiring, thin-necked man with grape-stained fingers. He looked an awful lot like a camel.

She turned to the others and pointed at the man. She twisted her mouth into a rubbery, pouty-lipped muzzle. Teeth bared, she began to chew an imaginary cud.

The other kids giggled while the men argued on without noticing.

It was Nathan's turn. He studied the potter's tight, woolly curls and thick, stubby neck. Nathan turned his head, forced a cough, and stuck out his tongue, mimicking the silent bleating of a stupid sheep.

Mara couldn't help it. Laughter burst out of her

mouth with all the grace of a busted vase.

Unfortunately, the adults chose that exact moment to catch their breath. The sound of Mara's hoarse snort filled the room.

Her mother glared at her. Mara's cheeks burned. She was going to get the "lady lecture" later, for sure. *I wonder if the governor's wife ever scratches or burps?* Mara thought. *I bet she does.*

The arguments resumed, and after sitting still for a few minutes, Mara slipped carefully and quietly to the back of the room. The other New Israel kids faded back too. She gave them a nod, and they made their escape.

Outside, the members of New Israel poked and wrestled each other, glad to be free.

"If Jesus had been that boring," Sarah said, dancing away from the boys, "nobody would have listened!"

"But He wasn't," Mara said in a superior tone. "He told great stories and let kids sit on His lap. I wish He was still here."

The others nodded. Jesus had shaken everybody up, sometimes with miracles but mostly just with words. People couldn't stop talking about Him.

As soon as they were out of earshot of the

adults, Mara gave the signal and Obadiah placed his index fingers against the gaps in his teeth and blew a piercing whistle. Immediately, the others left their horseplay and fell in behind Mara, who led them in the club theme song.

"We are New Israel, kids of strength and might;
Messiah has favored us, given us new light!
Do not get in our way or we will stand and fight.
We stand the test, 'cause we're the best.
We know that we are right!"

"Obadiah sang it wrong again, Mara," complained Nathan, checking to see that his orange and brown striped cloak hadn't gotten smudged. His mother had woven the wool on her loom and colored it with special dye. Nathan was very careful about his clothes.

"Did not!" objected Obadiah, his considerable roundness covered by a red and blue cloak.

"Oh, yes, you did," corrected Nathan. "You ended with 'tight' instead of 'right,' like you always do."

"Look, Mr. Perfection," Obadiah said, "what difference does it make? We're right *and* tight, so what's the big deal?"

Nathan pulled his matching turban more firmly

into place over his mop of black hair. "The big deal is that I wrote the song and it's 'might,' 'light,' 'fight,' and 'right,' not 'tight.' Got it?"

"Bright," said Mara.

"Huh?" Nathan threw a confused look her way.

"Bright," said Mara again. "I think 'bright' is better. It's got 'right' in it, but it says more." She walked carefully, staying in the lead. She was tall for her 11 years, and she considered herself practically a woman. *Wise, too*, she thought smugly.

"I like Mara's idea," said Obadiah. "We can use 'tight' in the first line."

" 'Kids of strength and *tight*'?" Nathan sneered. "You think about as well as you sing."

Obadiah growled. "My parents think I sing just fine."

"That's because your father's a bullfrog and your mother's a screech owl. I wrote the song and I ought to know the right word. And in this case the right word is 'right.' "

Mara had had enough. "Stop it! It's a stupid argument and you know it!"

"We're not arguing," sniffed Nathan; "we're—" One look at Mara's face and he realized he'd better not finish the sentence.

Mara began walking again, trying to imagine herself away from there. She strode the dark, narrow streets of the Old City as if she owned them. Sometimes she imagined that she owned the whole city—every merchant's stall, every official's marbled home, every fine steed in the Roman stables.

Her bearing was tall, her chin strong. Her dark eyes flashed with the fire of leadership. And she was beautiful. Her father said so. Sarah's aunt thought she must have a royal branch in her family tree. Mara liked Sarah. Sarah didn't say much.

One day Mara would have the respect of the whole city. For now, she was the leader of New Israel. She was proud of their club for *true* Hebrew Christian kids. The Jewish kids from Greece and Cyprus and other foreign places who had moved to Jerusalem would just have to form their own club. They didn't even speak Aramaic—they chattered away about their strange beliefs in Greek! Mara had to admit that one of the reasons she didn't like them was because the foreigners were the cause of half the arguments in the church.

She adjusted the fine, white cloth of her meeting dress and patted her pale-pink head veil. It flowed over raven-black hair that reached halfway down her back.

She straightened and felt that she must look regal. Maybe she would be queen of an entire country one day.

"Must you walk like an ostrich?" Nathan asked. A year younger and six inches shorter than Mara, he acted like he owned the rule book. He spent his school days with the teachers of the Law called rabbis. Most of the time he came home sounding like them.

"Go away, baby rabbi," Mara said. "I'm thinking."

Nathan did not go away. "You need to respect the males of your family. We can teach you many things."

Mara patted him on the turban. "You barely wash behind your ears. You ought to listen more and speak less."

Nathan looked at her with indignant brown eyes. She knew what was coming. "In synagogue school, we're taught that female children should master the skills of the home and proper ways of cooking. They should not make fun of teachings they know nothing about."

"Speaking of cooking, did you finish off the cinnamon flat bread I baked for Father?" Mara accused, suddenly suspicious.

"Someone had to." Nathan shrugged, but his face broke into a sly grin. "I couldn't allow Father to be poisoned."

Mara looked at him and frowned. "I liked you better when you were the size of a squirrel and had the vocabulary of a centipede."

"Centipedes can't talk," Nathan retorted.

"Exactly."

They arrived shortly at the cool, sheltering walls of the Pool of Siloam. The sweet waters of the Gihon Spring flowed through the tunnel that good King Hezekiah had dug into Jerusalem beneath the city wall. The shaded pool made a perfect meeting place for their club.

The New Israelites knelt by the pool and drank the refreshing water from cupped hands.

Mara was about to call the meeting to order when she noticed someone slouched in the dark recesses of the tunnel's mouth. A shiver slithered down her regal spine.

It's Karis the river rat. What's she doing here? she thought in annoyance.

"Eeewwww! What's that smell? I think it's coming from something in that moldy old tunnel." Sarah pointed at the figure in the shadows.

"Yeah, it stinks like old garlic and rotten olives," said Obadiah. He held his nose and stomach and lurched about as if he would lose his breakfast.

Karis emerged cautiously from the tunnel. Her hands were behind her, hiding something.

The New Israel kids shrieked in mock terror.

"It's the girl from the ground!"

"The brat from below!"

"Yes, yes . . . it's the Dung Hole Detective!"

Karis's shoulders slumped. She was plain and small for her age. Barefoot, clothed in a shapeless, frayed cloak of drab brown, the girl from Caesarea-by-the-Sea had been in Jerusalem less than a year. Mara felt sorry for her in a way. She knew Karis just wanted to be friends with the New Israelites. She wanted to feel close to the Hebrews who had seen Jesus and heard Him speak.

On the other hand, Karis was always boasting about what an explorer she was. How back home in Caesarea she knew every square inch of the vast underground sewer system built by Herod the Great. She was as proud of poking around in the dark, smelly old tunnels as the Egyptians were of building their pyramids. It was embarrassing! Plus she tied her dull black hair on top of her head in a sorry little knot resembling a dead animal.

Still, Mara felt a moment's guilt. What if she were in Karis's place and unaccepted by others—a foreigner? Karis's family was penniless, supported only by what the church could spare.

Well, it's their own fault, Mara thought impatiently. No one had forced them to leave Caesarea and move to Jerusalem, where unemployment—especially for believers of the Way—was high. Surely they had relatives they could go back to. Mara had to look after her own. She was the head of New Israel, after all. She was born in Jerusalem. Her father was a respected architect, a leader in the church, and her family had money. God must have wanted it that way.

"What are you hiding behind your back?" Mara demanded, speaking the Greek all the educated Hebrew children were taught along with their native Aramaic. "Show us."

Karis, less schooled and unable to speak Aramaic, was outnumbered but wiry and quick. Mara watched her closely. If she'd discovered something valuable while traveling the tunnels, it wouldn't do to frighten her or they'd never get to see it.

"I don't think you want to know what's in here,"

Karis said, bringing a rough woven sack into view.

"You'll never be allowed to join New Israel if you don't learn to cooperate," said Mara. But she was thinking, *It'd be easier for you to stuff a camel through the eye of a needle than to get into this club.*

Mara shuddered. The thought of Karis climbing around underground through dangerous, scary places gave her the creeps. But she wasn't about to let Karis get away with saying no to the leader of New Israel.

"Okay, don't say you weren't warned." Karis stepped forward and the curious members of the club crowded around. Mara leaned over for a better look. Karis held her arms straight out and opened the top of the sack.

A severed calf's head lay in the bottom of the bag and its unseeing right eye caught the light so that it seemed to wink at them. Blue flies crawled over the dead face. A reeking aroma flooded the kids' noses and made their eyes water.

"That's awful!" Mara shouted and jumped back.

Karis laughed. "Not as awful as a person who sticks her head in a sack before she knows what's in it—*that's* just stupid!"

"She makes a pretty good point," said Nathan.

"Be quiet!" Mara snapped. She took two steps

forward and wagged a finger under Karis's nose. "Don't call me stupid!" she yelled. "I'm not the one walking around with my brains in a bag!"

"It's *not* brains!"

"Is too! What do you think that calf's got between its ears, sister?"

"The same thing you do—nothing! And don't call me 'sister'!"

"You're taking that home so your mother can make boiled calf's brains for supper. That's what poor people eat!"

Mara was sorry the second she said it, but there was no way to take it back. *A real queen would never speak to her subjects that way—even the strange ones*, she thought.

Karis looked at the ground. Mara felt a moment's regret. These were hard times for followers of Messiah. Timon, Karis's father, was one of the seven men appointed by the church to help the widows and others who struggled. But it was only a volunteer position. Maybe a calf's head for supper was all Karis's family could afford.

Mara's embarrassing words hung in the air until she suggested that the club members get going. "We'll have the meeting at my house, okay?" The others mumbled in response and started to leave.

"Wait!" Karis called to them. "I'm sorry. That was mean. I should have told you what was in the bag first. Do you want to see my new twin goat kids? They suckle your fingers and have the cutest little white circles around their eyes!"

The New Israelites stopped and looked at Mara. Their faces said they wanted to see the baby goats. She hesitated, unsure of how she felt about this smudged girl who smelled of damp and dirty places. But she was sure of how she felt about baby animals. She loved them. One day she would own a royal game park and raise all the babies by hand.

"I guess so," Mara said. "Just keep that sack away from me."

Karis brightened. "Great! This way." She started toward the tunnel entrance.

Mara and the others halted. "Not in there," Mara said.

"But the goats are grazed outside the city walls by a friend of ours," said Karis. "Come on. I'll show you."

"Let's go out through the city gate," Mara insisted.

"You're not scared, are you?" Karis challenged. "I can find my way through these tunnels blindfolded."

"We're not scared," said Mara, giving Nathan a look guaranteed to keep him quiet. "We're wearing our nice meeting clothes and we don't want to come out smelling of dead fish."

That was true, but Mara knew that Karis knew the whole truth: The New Israel kids were frightened to go underground. The dark, winding passages were tight and smelly. It was too easy to get lost in them. The kids had all heard horrible tales of terrifying creatures and of children who wandered into the tunnels never to be seen again. Mara suspected the stories were made up to protect the kids from accidents. If so, the stories worked.

Karis sighed, shouldered her sack, and reentered Hezekiah's tunnel. "Suit yourself," she said, "but I came this way and I'm going back this way." The words sounded deep and hollow, as if they came from the bottom of a barrel. The dark tunnel swallowed Karis first, followed by the rough brown sack with the calf's head inside.

Mara shuddered. Karis could just forget about her goats. Who wanted to hang out with a girl who liked dark places and carried dead things on her back?

CHAPTER 2

Let's run!" Nathan yelled to Obadiah. "We'll meet you girls at the nut merchant's stall by the western temple wall. Last one there's a rotten pomegranate!"

Off they raced. Mara shook her head and watched them take the first corner in perfect stride . . . right into an angry tide of people rushing toward them. Shouting and cursing, the mob was pulling a familiar-looking man down the street by a rope that bound his wrists together.

Mara caught up to the boys and snatched Nathan out of the crowd by the belt of his robe.

"He mocks the temple!" cried one sweating accuser, so upset that blood dribbled from his lips. Apparently, he had chewed them in fury.

Others shouted, "The Sanhedrin rulers know what to do with this mocker!"

Mara trembled and could feel Nathan trembling too. Sarah looked ready to faint. She could talk pretty bravely, but she was thin and sick a lot of the time. Now, even her freckles were pale. Mara put an arm around her shoulders.

New Israel never wanted to fall into the hands of the Sanhedrin. They were stern men with beards longer than anyone else's. They judged disagreements among the Jews, and their word was final. People who scorned the temple died.

As the mob passed, Mara looked closely at the kind, bearded face in the middle of the stampede. The man's wrists were swollen from the rope. *Stephen! It's Stephen! But he's famous in the church. Why's he being yanked along like an animal?*

This wasn't the first time something like this had happened. Jesus had also been shoved through town on His way to the cross.

"Stone him! Stone him!" The terrible cry came from every direction. Mara covered her ears. *"Crucify him! Crucify him!"* That's what they'd said. *I was a little girl then. His face was kind like Stephen's. He smiled at me. I know He did,* she thought.

Nathan glanced anxiously at his sister. Obadiah

yanked nervously at his cloak. Sarah looked as if she'd swallowed a big cup of sour milk. Mara could see that the rest of New Israel didn't want to be there either.

Suddenly, there was Karis across the way, standing back among the camels and mules laden for market. *What's she doing here?* Mara watched the girl's mouth try to form words, but they seemed frozen on her lips. The sack on her back slipped from her fingers and fell into the street.

A bull camel with sad, droopy eyes and an even sadder, droopier hump did not like the shouting and commotion. It reared away from the angry scramble. What looked like 400 pounds of market goods tied to its back swayed precariously from side to side. The creature and its load nearly backed into Karis, spilling a crate of grapes in the process.

The camel stamped and kicked and sent grapes flying in every direction.

Karis stumbled sideways. The beast's wide, dirty foot landed on the sack. The camel's weight smashed the calf's head inside.

Mara dodged the procession and rushed over to Karis. She started to scold, but then she said, a little more kindly than she felt, "Are you okay?"

Karis nodded, but her face was pale. "That's Stephen. What are they doing to him?" she asked in Greek.

Mara ignored the question. She didn't want to hear the answer herself. Instead, she fished in the pocket of her gown and said, "It looks like your dinner is ruined. I have a few coins. You can have boiled mustard greens for supper."

From the look on Karis's face, Mara guessed that Karis hated boiled mustard greens. So did Mara. *But more than boiled calf's brains?* she wondered. *No way!* She shrugged and left the coins in her pocket.

The noisy crowd had passed up the street. A thick cloud of dust followed them. Each time Stephen slowed to speak to someone who dared ask what was going on, he was jerked forward by the rope. "Why are they so mad at him?" Karis asked.

"They don't like what he says," answered a tall boy who appeared at Karis's elbow. He spoke Greek and was one of the other foreign kids who had attended the meeting of the Way. Mara figured they must have gotten sick of the meeting too. Three more stood with him. "I heard he bad-mouthed Moses. God, too!"

Nathan, Obadiah, and the other New Israelites joined Mara.

"That's crazy," Obadiah said. Eyes hard with suspicion, he stared at the tall boy. "Stephen just helps little old ladies. I heard that what makes him really different is he does miracles!"

The tall boy shrugged. "Nawh, he thinks Jesus changed everything, even the Law. He's right. Nothing around here's been the same since Jesus came."

The New Israelites gasped. "Hey, what do you mean?" Obadiah demanded. "The Law has been around forever."

"Yes," said Nathan, who was overexcited and close to tears. "It came from Moses. Moses wrote the Torah. Torah teaches us how to live." He shook his finger in the boy's face. "You take it back or I'll report *you* to the Sanhedrin!"

"Stop it!" said Mara. She didn't like this talk one bit. She switched to Aramaic so the foreign kids couldn't understand what she was saying to New Israel. "We are the true Jews. We knew Jesus. Don't let these outsiders ruin things for us!"

The New Israel club members nodded. Then they glared at the nonmembers.

"Stop talking in your secret code," Karis said.

She put her hands on her hips and glared at Mara. "If you're so smart, you should speak Greek and not talk behind our backs!"

"If you were smart," Obadiah shouted back in Greek, "you could speak *two* languages, like we can. But instead, you wear garlic perfume and stink like camel dung!"

"Oh, that was helpful, Obadiah," said Mara, wrinkling her nose.

"Yeah, helpful as a broken leg!" added the tall boy.

Mara thought his name was Akbar. He was dark and from somewhere along the Nile River in Egypt. He could be nice. Sometimes. Right now he was clenching his fists and looking ready to punch someone.

"At least I don't *look* like a pile of camel dung!" Karis finally said, although she looked more like she wanted to cry than to name-call.

"Good one, Karis!" Akbar's encouragement made her smile a little.

Nathan stepped between the two groups, hands folded, face serious, looking for all the world like a miniature Pharisee. Mara groaned. She could guess what was coming.

Nathan cleared his throat. "In synagogue school, Torah teaches that we must learn to live with our neighbors. Because you foreigners have moved to Jerusalem to live, you must learn to live with us. We're your new neighbors. The Law is good. The Law is life."

The other New Israelites clapped and cheered the speech as Mara rolled her eyes. The foreigners stuck their tongues out at them.

"Thank you, Nathan, that was just what we needed," said Mara sarcastically.

"I try," Nathan replied, trying to look as wise as possible and missing her sarcasm.

"Put a sandal in it, little brother!" Mara grabbed Nathan, shoved him to the back, and took his place.

"I feel dizzy," said Sarah, sitting down on a packing crate. Mara fanned her face and tried to ignore the camel that was standing nearby, coughing and showing his yellow teeth.

"If you're *our* neighbors, then who are *yours?*" Akbar demanded.

The camel looked sour and ready to spit.

"What are you saying?" Obadiah asked.

"I'm saying, who do *you* have to learn to live with? Or does your Law go only one way?"

"The Law *is* the way," Obadiah sneered. "Why don't you go back to Egypt or Caesarea or wherever you came from? The sun has baked your heads until nothing's left inside!" The New Israelites thumped him on the back and stuck their tongues out at the foreigners.

Karis trembled and looked angry. "I wish I *could* go back. It's no fun to live in a city with kids like you. You are tiny Jews with faith as small as grains of dirt. I have more faith between my toes!"

She turned and started home. Akbar and the others marched off beside her.

Obadiah had heard enough. He bent down and scooped up three bunches of fat grapes from the ground. He threw one at Karis's back. It landed between her shoulder blades with a satisfying splat.

"Outsider!" Obadiah sneered again.

Karis spun, snatched up a grape, and let it fly. Obadiah ducked and it missed. When he straightened, Akbar's grapes caught him in the arm and smeared juice and pulp from elbow to wrist.

Grapes filled the air. So did name-calling.

"Mule!"

"Maggot!"

"Cockroach!"

"Sewer beetle!"

"Lawbreaker!" Nathan looked pleased with the sound of that one.

Akbar slipped on some grape skins and fell knees first into donkey droppings. Fresh ammunition.

But just then a boy ran up to the war zone and shouted, "They're taking Stephen outside the city walls. Come on!"

The war ended as quickly as it had begun. The whole group, Mara and her friends and Karis and hers, ran after the boy.

They arrived together, breathless and splattered and quite unprepared for the awful sight they saw.

CHAPTER 3

Stephen's crumpled body lay at the bottom of the rock quarry. He had been pushed from the edge 30 feet above. This was to show "mercy," since the condemned man would already be half dead from the fall before the stones came raining down on his body.

Several men were reaching for stones. Others had large chunks raised above their heads, ready to strike.

Mara felt cold and sick.

"We'd better go," suggested Sarah, but no one moved.

The stones fell, Stephen moaned, and Mara covered her eyes.

A young man stood apart from the others, tall and stern. He studied the executioners and watched the stoning closely. Once in a while he nodded approval.

"It's Saul of Tarsus," whispered Obadiah, out of breath. "Stephen's not the first Christian he's killed."

"I thought only the Roman governor could execute a person," Karis protested. "We've got to tell somebody!" Tears ran down her face, mingling with the grape stains.

"Shhh, quiet," said Akbar. "Do you want them to hear you? It wouldn't take much of a rock to shut you up!"

"He's right," Mara said, hugging herself to keep from shaking. "There's nothing we can do."

"Poor Stephen," Karis whimpered. "He helped my dad care for the poor and he brought us food. He gave me sweet figs to eat. He and my father talked about Jesus for hours."

The dull thud of rock striking flesh made them cringe. The condemned man groaned. The kids groaned. The crowd hushed. Mara wondered if any of them were sorry they were getting what they had asked for.

"You children should not be here!"

Mara jumped. A short, squatty man glared at her. "Run away!" he scolded, shooing her off with a pudgy hand. "There's going to be trouble. This won't be the end of it, you'll see!"

He almost spat at her. Mara backed away and motioned the others to higher ground.

From a little hill of rubble, they watched the sweating men bending down for more rocks, their faces full of heat and hate.

Mara prayed for a miracle. *God, don't let Stephen die!* She reached for Nathan. He wasn't there.

"Nathan! Where's Nathan?" Panic gripped Mara.

"He was here a minute ago," said Obadiah, breathing hard.

"Nathan!" called Mara. "Nathan!"

"Here. Here, Mara!" Nathan scrambled up the rocky mound. Dirt streaked his sweaty face.

"You mud ball!" she scolded. But she couldn't hide the relief in her voice. "Where were you?"

"I wanted to get nearer to Saul of Tarsus, but he was swearing and threatening every member of the Way. I think he wants to kill us all!"

Mara shivered and pulled her brother close.

"Look!" Karis cried. "He's getting up!"

They all watched as Stephen, horribly bloodied,

staggered to his feet. His lips moved and a hush fell over the crowd.

He looked toward heaven. His expression was one of pain mixed with peace. Loudly, he cried, "Lord Jesus, receive my spirit!"

He stumbled and dropped to his knees. He cried out again, "Lord, do not hold this sin against them!" Then he collapsed and was still.

Mara looked at Saul, who was watching the body for signs of life. There weren't any.

He forgave his murderers! Mara couldn't believe it. Jesus had done the same thing on the cross.

"How could he forgive those people?" Obadiah asked, an angry look on his face. "They killed him." He shook his head. "I couldn't forgive them."

"Me either," said Sarah, tears streaming down her face.

"Come on," Mara said, an ache in her throat. "We need to go back." They left the quarry, their heads hanging, tears streaking paths through the dirt on their faces.

Nobody talked much on the way home until Nathan finally said quietly, "In synagogue school, the rabbis teach that it's right for you to forgive someone up to three times."

"Some of those men threw a lot more than three rocks," Obadiah said angrily.

"Jesus said to forgive 70 times 7, if you have to," Akbar said. He sounded anything but ready to do that.

"He meant we shouldn't keep track," Mara said shakily. "We should just forgive whenever someone says he's sorry."

"But none of Stephen's murderers said they were sorry." Obadiah practically spat the words. Then he sniffled and lowered his head to hide his tears. "He asked the Lord to forgive them anyway. I don't think I could have done that," he finished quietly.

"He was different. We're supposed to be different too. We're the Way, followers of Messiah," Karis said in a dull voice. Her face was gray as ash.

Gloom settled over them. They walked slowly. Mara was afraid to think what she was thinking. For the first time since her family had put their trust in the Way of Jesus, she wondered if it was such a good idea.

Then Nathan spoke her thoughts aloud. "I don't feel safe anymore." He looked as if he might cry.

"What do you mean?" his sister asked, afraid of what he would say.

"I mean, who's next? What if Saul decides to hunt down the rest of us? Where could we hide?"

Mara had no answer. *Where* could *we hide?* she wondered.

They all looked scared. Really scared.

Mara tried to forget what they'd just seen. To make her back straight again, like a queen's. To walk her royal walk. The truth was, though, she felt about as royal as a flattened grape.

She knew that the memory of that awful stoning would never leave their heads. Stephen's words repeated again and again in her mind: *"Lord, do not hold this sin against them."*

Mara tried instead to think of the New Israel theme song. But she couldn't remember a single word. Even if she had been able to recall the words, there was no way she could possibly sing it.

CHAPTER 4

The next day, Mara's father, Joshua, called an emergency meeting of the Way. Joshua was a leader in the new church.

Mara loved to watch him. He was tall, strong, and handsome. He looked like royalty. When he spoke, people stopped their chatter and listened closely. His voice, deep and clear, commanded attention. Today it made heads shake, lips tremble, and mothers clutch their babies tighter. As Mara listened, she felt proud and petrified at the same time.

"Believers in Jesus, listen! Stephen's death will not be the last! In the night, Saul's thugs broke into John's and Justin's homes, taking them and their sons captive. Six more, friends. Six *more*!" A shudder passed through the crowd in the main room of Mara's house.

As soon as the emergency meeting of the Way

had been called, Mara had called an emergency meeting of New Israel. Karis and a bunch of her friends had come with their parents and wanted to sit with New Israel. Mara was annoyed. *Can't they form their own club?*

Most of the kids, whether in or out of New Israel, had a younger brother or sister to watch. Sarah had two little sisters. The children stood bunched together in the hot room, made hotter each time one more person squeezed into the back.

People filled the room. Fear filled the air. The babies felt it and fussed. Mara felt it and her knees shook.

"I knew it!" It was the short, squat man who had frightened the children at the quarry. "I knew we shouldn't start separating ourselves and calling ourselves 'believers.' People think we're different. It makes us look suspicious!"

"We *are* different!" cried a bent old man with a long, white beard. Many others nodded. "We know Jesus is the Messiah. He was sent by God to help us, and men like Saul killed Him to shut Him up. Now they've killed Stephen, too. It's not going to end there!" People raised their voices in fear, and chaos threatened to ensue.

"Keep your voices down!" Joshua said in a fierce whisper.

Mara was worried. Her father, who usually looked calm and collected, now looked awfully scared. For the first time in her life, Mara didn't know if even he could keep their family safe.

"Where'd they take the brothers?" Timon, Karis's father, inquired.

"To prison!" another man answered from the crowd.

"On what charge?"

"That they encouraged others to quit the old ways and to begin anew."

That started another argument. Faces flushed in anger. Fingers pointed.

"Please, my friends, no fighting," Joshua urged, trying to bring peace. He spoke in Greek so that all would understand. "This is not about who's right and who's wrong. Our lives are in danger. We've got to have a plan!"

Mara tensed. Sometimes she thought her father spent too much time trying to include the Greeks in everything. Let them look after themselves. In fact, let them get their own church. They could worship in their own odd way, eat their own funny food, and

jabber away in their own language. Leave the Hebrew believers to worship, eat, and speak according
to the ways and laws handed down from long ago.
For hundreds and hundreds of years, she thought,
*we true Jews have kept our ways of thinking and
worshiping. It's what makes us special. Jesus is* our
Messiah!

"Whatever the plan," her father continued,
"we've got to be prepared to go to jail. Don't think
being a law-abiding citizen will save you. Saul
doesn't need an excuse. He isn't concerned about the
truth. He thought Jesus was a troublemaker, and he
thinks we're just as bad."

"Since when is believing in God's Son a crime?"
the white-bearded old gentleman asked.

"Punishable by stoning to death?" piped up the
short, squat man.

"It's because we call sin what it is," cried another. "That makes us dangerous."

When Joshua had them quieted once again, he
said, "What makes us really dangerous is that we
don't put our trust in priests or governors. We trust
in Jesus, the One who died for our sins! But for that,
friends, we will suffer."

Her father's words upset Mara more. She hated

feeling angry and scared and confused all at once. She wished she could forget the nightmare in her mind of poor Stephen bloody and dying. She didn't want her family or friends to suffer. What if that had been her father being stoned?

Mara dug her fingernails deep into the palms of her hands. It was too horrible to imagine. And too unfair. If Saul wanted to throw somebody in jail who was really different, why didn't he pick on Karis the tunnel girl? Now *there* was a weird person.

She felt a jab in the ribs. It was Karis's elbow. Mara glared at the other girl. Karis glared right back. "Why'd you poke me?" Mara demanded.

"Because you deserve to be poked—and worse!" Karis almost growled. "Haven't you been listening to your father? Of course not. You think you're too good for most people. You give the Way a bad name. You and your slave of a brother!"

Now Karis had two people glaring at her.

"You take that back, you overgrown water bug!" growled Nathan, making a fist. "I'll show you who's a slave!"

Karis was as jumpy as the rest, but it didn't hide her disgust. "Saul could come here and take us any minute, but you still want to pick fights. Baby rabbis don't go around slugging people, unless of course they're looking for work on the Sanhedrin!" She turned away.

Nathan sputtered but relaxed his fist. "Good thing for you Torah doesn't let me punch a girl," he muttered at her back.

"Does it let you punch a boy?" Suddenly, Akbar practically stood on Nathan's toes, and the look on his face said it wasn't a friendly visit.

Mara grabbed Nathan. Sarah grabbed Mara. Obadiah bumped into Akbar, belly first, ready to defend Nathan. No member of New Israel looked happy. No nonmember of New Israel looked happy. No one else in the room looked happy either.

Mara hadn't been paying attention to what was going on in the room, so she was surprised when a chunk of stale bread suddenly sailed from somewhere over the heads of the crowd. The bread nearly landed in a clay pot that was filled with lamp oil and sitting on a bench near the fireplace at the center of the room. Two young men at the front of the room stood chin to chin, ready to tear each other's beards out.

Forgetting his own warning to keep it down,

Joshua bellowed, "Stop it! Animals behave better than this!"

Startled, the men released each other's clothing and took a step back. Some people looked embarrassed. All looked uneasy. They turned to Joshua.

"Would Jesus be pleased with us?" he asked, arms spread to include everyone.

The people shrank back, murmuring to themselves. Mara, Karis, and the others stared at the floor.

Suddenly, the door burst open with a crash. Mara stood frozen to the spot as five men she'd never seen before stormed the meeting, swinging clubs and lunging for anyone they could grab. Screams and shouts and the shrieking of children turned the room into a madhouse.

The bench toppled to the floor, dumping lamp oil with a splash. The oil caught fire, but a man quickly stamped it out. Mara watched her pretty, hand-woven fruit basket fall beneath stampeding feet. Two huge clay water pitchers fell from the shelf and broke against the floor in a thousand pieces. *Mother will be sick. Where is she?* Mara wondered. She tried to see through the crowd, but all was confusion.

People shoved and crawled for the doorway. The cows and chickens at the front of the house bawled and squawked in terror.

Mara searched frantically for her father. He was wrestling one of the attackers, trying to yank the thick wooden club out of his hand. What could she do?

A shriek from Obadiah's little sister made up Mara's mind. She would save the kids and pray that her father and mother could get away.

Separated from their parents by the intruders in the confusion, the children looked dazed. Mara pushed and herded four of the youngest out the door to the street. Sarah had one in each hand and a third on her back. The older boys followed with the rest.

"Quick!" Mara ordered. "To the roof! Hurry!"

She carried and pulled four children up the stone stairs beside the house. After she'd shoved them onto the roof, she reached back for the others running up the stairs behind her and pushed them forward. Karis joined them and with the older boys made everyone lie flat against the roof.

Mara peered over the edge and watched the men and women, her parents included, being herded down the street like cattle. Other people stopped to watch the spectacle and point at the prisoners.

"Where'd those kids go?" one of the attackers shouted from the street.

"We'll come for them later," shouted the one in the lead. "They can't hide forever."

The last thing Mara saw before they turned the corner was her father looking back toward the roof. He knew she would hide up there. It was where she'd loved to go as a little girl. She'd take her pet lamb and watch it graze in the grass that grew in the mud and clay roof. *Jesus, Messiah, don't let them hurt Mother and Father.* Without thinking, she started to raise a hand to wave, but Nathan yanked it down.

"Saul's men!" Nathan warned. "They've taken our parents, Mara. They've taken *all* our parents!"

The little ones looked wide-eyed and stunned. Mara put her finger to her lips and Nathan grew quiet.

"I think we should pray," Mara said. She looked at Nathan.

"I can't," Nathan said in a small voice, then started to cry.

Mara felt the cold of the empty house below come right up through the roof into her heart. "They'll be back for us," she said. "We'd *better* pray!"

CHAPTER 5

We have to get away from here, Mara thought. *Saul's men will come back. And when they do, they won't think twice about hurting us.*

Though it was a hot day, she felt chilled all over. Her pretty royal dreams were gone. The memory of sharp rocks raining down on Stephen's head and body tormented her. Would the same thing happen to her parents and the others? How long would it take for rocks to finish off her mother and father?

Mara tried to think of what to do. The kids of New Israel crowded around. Their little sisters and brothers cried. The harder she tried to quiet them, the louder they bawled.

She looked into her brother's tear-streaked face. He rubbed his eyes with his fists and tried to pretend he hadn't been crying. "I want Mom and Dad."

"I know, Nathan, I know!" she murmured,

putting a comforting arm around his shoulders. "I'm trying to think of something . . ."

She looked at Karis at the other end of the roof trying to comfort the others. Their cries were getting steadily louder as the children began to realize what had happened. Soon they would be heard from the street. It was hopeless.

Karis came over and frowned at Mara. "We aren't safe here," she said, stating the obvious.

"I know that!" Mara hissed.

"So what's the plan?" Karis hissed right back. "You got us up here!"

"And I'll get us down!" Mara insisted forcefully, though she didn't feel forceful. Getting down was the easy part. What then?

She thought frantically, *What do I do now? The neighbors don't believe in Jesus. They never have liked us holding meetings in our house. They must know we're up here. They might turn us in.*

"Well?" Karis demanded.

"We can climb that giant olive tree in the Garden of Gethsemane and hide out in the branches."

"Right," said Karis sarcastically. "And we can make like olives—they'll never guess we're really kids!"

"Yeah," Akbar joined in. "If we painted Obie a dark green-black, he could pass for the world's biggest olive!"

"You take that back or I'll give you an 'olive' right between the eyes!" Obadiah pulled a wicked-looking slingshot from his cloak and scanned the roof for suitable ammunition.

"Would you two knock it off!" Mara yelled, forgetting to be quiet. "Obie, put that thing away. Can't you see the kids are scared enough as it is?"

"You don't have a clue what we should do, do you?" Karis put in. "I thought the leader of New Israel knew everything!"

"She's trying, Karis," Sarah said, arms tight around her sniffling little sisters. "Please give her a chance."

Mara smiled gratefully at Sarah and ignored Karis. "I've got it! We'll go to the Dead Sea and hide out in the caves. Nobody'll find us there!"

"Including our parents," Akbar snorted. "You can get lost in those caves."

"It's a bad idea," Karis agreed. "They'll be watching the city gates. Besides, it's 15 miles to the Dead Sea. How far do you think we'll get with those?" She pointed to the short, chubby legs of

Obadiah's four-year-old sister.

"About half a mile," sniffled Nathan.

Mara gave her brother a whose-side-are-you-on? look. "Do you have a better idea?" she asked Karis.

"As a matter of fact, I do. Follow me."

The New Israelites looked at Mara for guidance. She hesitated a moment. She didn't know what to do, and Karis seemed to have a plan. Surrendering her pride, she nodded.

The children streamed down from the roof, Karis in the lead. She darted from doorway to doorway, and they darted after her in twos and threes like hesitant shadows.

A woman yelled from a window, "Where are you going? Come back here!"

They ran as if wild dogs snapped at their heels. They grabbed and pulled one another along, the older carrying the younger. When some stumbled, others picked them up. All ignored scraped knees and torn clothing.

When Sarah started to fall behind with her little sisters, Obadiah and Akbar carried the little girls. If they saw a commotion or a group of men in the main street, the children squirted away down a side alley. At one turn they panicked when a ragged man pointed a bony finger their way and shouted, "Run-aways! Somebody stop them!" But they were gone in an instant. If an alley looked too dark or danger-ous, they stuck to the main street, trying to act like children at play, as if nothing was wrong.

But plenty was wrong, Mara knew. There was tension in the city. People hurried along and looked at each other with suspicion. There wasn't the usual market-day laughter and excitement. Even the noisy beggars were silent. She half expected to see a wanted poster painted on the side of the fish market: "Reward for Believers in Jesus—Dead or Alive!" Even the stiff fish in the baskets they passed seemed to look at her with accusing eyes.

It was only then that she noticed Karis was cup-ping a three-inch clay lamp in one hand. A tiny flame flickered at its tip.

"Hey, where'd you get that?" Mara demanded. "That's one of my mother's olive oil lamps. You stole it from my house!"

"We'll need light where we're going. Mine ran out of oil. Besides, it was a little hard to ask your permission in the middle of a war!"

Suddenly, Karis slipped down a narrow passage where sunlight never penetrated. "Come on!" she motioned them to follow between the buildings. "It's this way."

When they caught up with her, Karis was lifting two paving stones from the side of the passage. Before Mara could say a word, Karis's bottom half disappeared into the gap between the stones. "It's all right," she said. "I'll help you down. Mara comes first, then the little ones, then you bigger boys. It's wet down there and you'll have to crawl a ways on your knees, but soon you'll be able to stand. Hand me the lamp once I'm down." She dropped from sight.

The kids hung back, even the ones banned from New Israel. The nonmembers liked Karis, but they did not like going underground.

"Come on, you guys," encouraged Mara shakily, determined not to quit. "She knows what she's doing. We've got to trust her. We're out of choices."

With that, Mara followed Karis into the hole and dropped with a splash onto her hands and knees in six inches of water. The slow-moving water swished past her, smelling like the damp dirt of an open grave. She fought back a scream and wound her soggy veil around her neck to keep it up. Her pretty gown soaked up water like a sponge. She pulled it above her knees.

"Thanks for trusting me." Karis's voice echoed in the tunnel. She set the lamp on a small ledge in the rock.

Mara glared at her. "You'd better know what you're doing."

Karis pointed in the direction of the moving water. "You'll want to go that way. The main tunnel's not far. You can stand up there and it's not as dark. Here, take the lamp." She handed Mara the light and reached up for Nathan, who insisted on not letting Mara out of his sight. He splashed down beside her. "Follow Mara," Karis instructed. "I'll send along the others."

One by one, the other children dropped into the tunnel with a splash, many of them whimpering and shivering from fright and the shock of the cold water. But when Karis said crawl, they crawled.

Mara sloshed forward into the darkness on one hand, her other hand holding the lamp safely above the water. The damp, musty smell of the cool air grew steadily stronger. She soon emerged into a taller and wider chamber where she could stand. The others popped from the side tunnel until they all stood in a tight circle around the comfort of the tiny, flickering flame.

"I'll take that," Karis said as she joined the group. Mara hesitated, then handed her the lamp.

"That tunnel leads to the north cistern," Karis explained, pointing back the way they'd come. "This is the main tunnel. That way"—she pointed downstream—"leads to the center of the business district out through the Pool of Siloam, where we met yesterday. That way"—she pointed upstream—"goes under the city wall and out of Jerusalem. We'll go that way. There's a place on the way where everyone can get out of the water and dry out. Then we can figure out what to do next.

"And one more thing." Her words bounced off the walls like startled bats. "As long as you're in my world, we talk in Greek, okay? I don't want any secrets down here." She looked right at Mara.

No one said anything, but someone coughed and they all jumped.

The place gave Mara the creeps. She should never have let the Dung Hole Detective lead New Israel to a watery grave. Her imagination began to conjure up images of the group wandering aimlessly through the tunnels for days, starving and forgotten.

What had she been thinking?

"Well?" Karis's one word echoed through the darkness with a dozen l's at the end. Mara bit back a scream.

She began to vigorously wring the water out of her gown to hide her nervousness. She squeezed the soggy end of her pretty cream-colored veil until it looked like a big wad of muck. Were the tunnels what really bothered her, or was it that Karis was in control?

"Okay," Mara said after a moment, "but you'd better be able to get us out of here!" Something wet plopped onto her shoulder from the ceiling and she jumped back, frantically trying to shake it off.

"Look, I know my way around down here," Karis said, flicking off the clump of mud that had fallen on Mara's shoulder. "You've got to trust me." The hand holding the lamp shook and made the reflection on the tunnel wall jerk around. "I'm worried about my parents too, you know. We've got to work together if we want to help them. While you've been playing queen for a day, I've been making a map up here of all the tunnels," she said as she tapped her forehead. "The perfect escape. Keep the little kids quiet and let's get going!"

"Hey!" Obadiah piped up in a shaky voice. "Who put you in charge?"

Karis shrugged. "You were too chicken to ever come down here before. And most of you didn't want me for a friend. But now what? Now you're in trouble and I'm all you've got. Let's be grateful one of us knows these tunnels."

The little ones had stopped sniffling. They were too frightened now to cry.

"Akbar, you take the lamp and the little kids and take the lead," Karis commanded. "You older kids stay in the back with me. I want you where I can see you."

"You don't trust us?" Obadiah asked.

"I don't trust you not to get lost," Karis said. "It looks like I'm responsible for keeping you alive, so would you please do as I ask?"

They went forward, but nobody talked except Karis, who gave Akbar directions. The floor began to slant slightly upward. The water rushed against their feet and ankles, and the footing was slippery. The walls of the passage narrowed until it was barely the width of an adult. Husky Obadiah had to shuffle along sideways. Sarah, just ahead of Mara, started breathing hard. Mara reached out a hand

and gave Sarah's elbow a comforting squeeze. She knew Sarah didn't like small spaces. Who did?

The lamp disappeared around a bend in the passage ahead, and those at the rear of the line were in almost total darkness. Mara's heart began beating faster and faster. The dark was where the monsters lived.

She rubbed against the slimy walls. It seemed like tons of rock were pressing in upon her. The farther they went, the sorrier she became that she had let Karis bring them all here. In the inky darkness, she could barely breathe.

"Karis," Akbar called back from the front of the line. The line stopped moving.

"What?" Karis replied.

"There's something here you should see."

"It can wait. We're almost there. The big chamber is only a little ways more. The tunnel widens out soon," Karis said.

"I-I think you'd better come look," Akbar called out shakily.

"What is it?"

"Come see."

Karis sighed and squeezed past Mara and the others. Now Mara was the last in line. In the pitch dark. *Dead last*, she thought.

She wished Karis hadn't left. There was comfort in knowing the other girl was behind her.

Suddenly, something cold and clammy clamped itself around her neck from behind. Mara screamed.

CHAPTER 6

Shhh!" Nathan's shaky voice sounded in her ear.

"Why did you sneak up on me like that?" Mara yelped, finding her brother's ear and giving it a yank. "I thought you were ahead of me."

"Ow! Let go of my ear! Can't you take a joke?"

"A joke? I'll tell you a joke. You're a joke!" Mara was furious. Her arms and legs felt like the water that swirled around her ankles.

"Calm down, Sis. The rabbis teach that a cool head and a sense of humor go together. You'll need that when you're queen."

Mara snorted.

"Queens don't snort," said Nathan. "They hire servants to snort for them."

She yanked his other ear.

"Ow! Cut it out! Do you want me to go around

with elephant ears because you couldn't control your yanking?"

Mara giggled nervously. *That* she couldn't control.

"What do you think they've found up there?" Nathan asked. He didn't have to wait long for the answer.

"Is everything okay back there?" Karis called out.

"Fine," answered Mara. "It's just my stinky brother acting his usual stinky self."

"Well, screams aren't a good idea right now," Karis called out in a shaky voice. She hesitated, then added, "We don't seem to be the only ones down here."

Mara's heart hammered. With Nathan shadowing her every step, she made her way to the head of the line.

They had reached the big chamber just as Karis had promised. At one end was the tunnel they had just entered by. At the other end, the passage left the big chamber and immediately branched into three separate tunnels. The place where they joined formed a wide floor slanted on the sides like the bottom of a bowl. Two of the tunnels produced slow streams of water. A small torrent rushed downhill toward them from the third, but the slanted sides rose above the water and formed a low shelf. As long as they stood on the shelf, they remained dry.

Karis was bending over something on the dry part of the floor. Then she stood up and stepped back. The others looked. It was a long arrow, hand-drawn in white chalk, pointing to the right-hand chamber.

"It's not yours, is it?" Mara questioned, her voice dry and barely more than a whisper. "You didn't draw it, did you?"

Karis shook her head but didn't say anything. Nathan peered around Mara and gulped. His face went pale as if he were staring at a poisonous snake set to strike. "They're hunting for us!"

"They're not hunting for us," Karis tried to reassure him. "But if they find us, we're in big trouble, no matter why they're down here."

"Look there," Akbar said as he pointed. A set of nearly dry footprints along the shelf disappeared into the darkness of the tunnel to the right from which water rushed.

"Don't tell us that's the way we have to go," Sarah whispered.

Karis nodded and held a finger to her lips in warning.

"Looks like you've gotten us trapped under-ground with the enemy!" Mara whispered furiously.

Karis held the lamp high and looked Mara in the eye. "We don't even know it's them," she whispered. "But if it *is* Saul and his men, they don't know these tunnels like *I* know these tunnels. That's why they had to mark the main branch so they wouldn't get lost. The other two tunnels dead-end at pools for collecting rainwater. Would you rather still be on that roof scared as rabbits waiting to be grabbed?"

"No, I'd much rather be stuck in a dark, smelly underground tunnel scared as rabbits waiting to be grabbed!" Mara shivered with fear and cold.

"Have a little faith and follow me," ordered Karis as she started back a short distance along the way they'd come. She dropped flat on her belly. There was a low opening at the bottom of the wall easily missed in the dim light. Only a very little water leaked from it. She wriggled through.

For a minute the others heard nothing. Mara was about to turn around and go back when the lamp showed at the opening. A hand slid out of the wall and motioned for them to follow.

Feeling as if she were going down, down, down to the center of the earth, Mara hesitated. Now that they were in the tunnels, they needed Karis to get them out. And they needed someplace where they could hide without Saul's men stumbling over them. If they ever saw the sun again, Mara would tell the girl from Caesarea just what she thought of her getting them all buried alive. But for now, she knew she had no choice.

Fuming, Mara helped the young ones crawl after Karis. She tried to make a quiet game of it so they wouldn't be so afraid. She murmured, "Little fish, little fish, swimming up the stream; slippery rocks, slippery rocks, we are all one team . . ." Like minnows, the youngest kids flopped and wiggled one by one into the opening and vanished from sight.

"I should have finished that grape fight while I had the chance!" Obadiah grumbled as he made his tight way through the hole.

"Shhh!" Mara shushed him but quickly stopped when the echo in the tunnel sounded louder than the original shush. It took some shoving from the others, but Obadiah finally made it with a groan and a relieved "Oof!"

Sarah followed, then Akbar. When it was

Nathan's turn, he put his mouth close to Mara's ear. "Queen Mara, promise me in your kingdom you'll have wide doors and high ceilings!"

Mara, the last through, crawled a short distance, then was helped out into a large, square room with sides 60 feet high. The walls were slimy and crumbling but thick enough that they could talk quietly without fear of attracting outside attention. A dim light filtered down from somewhere at the top of the walls. Karis walked over to four oil-soaked torches hung from the walls and lit them with the flame from the lamp. Then she blew out the little lamp to conserve oil.

The smoky light from the torches was welcome, although it showed just how bare their hideout was.

Nathan looked around and moaned. He pulled on Mara's arm. "This place isn't much better than a tomb!"

Karis frowned at them. "This would not be a good time to complain about the hideout. You have to admit, we're out of sight. It's a forgotten rain storage well that's been sealed over at the top. If we keep our voices down, nobody will know we're in here."

Mara gave Karis her best what-now? look.

Karis turned her back. "Let's catch our breath. Give me time to think." She plopped herself down against the wall, released her hair from the pins that had kept it in the pitiful little bun that Mara disliked, and closed her eyes. Absentmindedly, she chewed on a strand of hair.

Mara found a partially dry spot and sat down, back against the wall. Her gown was ruined. She thought of the hours her mother had put into the stitching. Her heart ached for home and her parents.

She heard a stirring of wings high above and thought she saw a shadow cross in front of a weak beam of light.

"Pigeons?" she asked hopefully.

"Bats," Karis replied, not opening her eyes.

Nathan clamped a hand tight over his sister's mouth.

After what seemed like hours, the little ones started crying quietly.

"I'm hungry."

"I'm cold."

"I feel sick."

"Can you take me to my mama now?"

"We're lost. When are we going to get out of here?"

The grumbling continued. Mara watched Karis for signs of life, but the girl sat apart from the others in stony silence, eyes closed. Was she thinking or sleeping?

Mara forced a cough. And another. And a third. But Karis, if she was conscious, didn't budge an eyelash.

"Maybe she's turned to salt," Nathan whispered.

"Maybe your brain has turned to mush," Mara said.

"My cloak sure has. Mother spent hours making this, and it only took minutes to ruin. Look at that." Nathan fingered the ragged edges of a large tear. "A hole you could drive a chariot through. Even if we make it out of here in one piece, I'm doomed."

"With a capital *D*," Mara agreed.

"We've got to do something."

"What would you suggest, O Wise One?"

Nathan huffed. "All I know is that if you ever get to be the queen, you're going to have to lead better than this."

The warning on Mara's face brought the conversation to a halt.

Some children whimpered for their mothers. Others slept. One of Sarah's little sisters pretended to hold a doll and sing to it. The silence lasted barely five minutes.

"Mara?"

"What, Nathan?"

"If you tell me the tooter rhyme, I'll tell you a joke."

Mara sighed. "I thought you learned serious, important things at synagogue school."

"Jokes are what I learn going to and from synagogue school. Please? I'm bored stiff. Two flute tooters tooted on a teeter-tooter..."

Mara stopped him. "Don't. You'll only mess it up like you always do. It goes like this: A tooter who tooted a flute tried to tutor two tutors to toot. Said the two to the tooter, 'Is it harder to toot or to tutor two tutors to toot?' "

Nathan laughed, stifling his snickers with both hands. No matter how many times he heard the rhyme, it always made him smile. Mara felt pleased to take his mind off their situation, even if just for a moment. "Your turn," she said warily.

He wore the silly grin he always did when telling dumb jokes.

Mara sighed. She was trapped.

"What belongs to you, but other people use it more than you do?"

"I give up."

"Your name."

"That's not a joke; it's a riddle."

"Okay, okay. Here's one. Why do bees hum?"

"I give up. Why?"

"Because they don't remember the words."

The little kids moved closer. Nathan had an audience.

"You give up too quickly," he told his sister. "This time, you have to think about it."

"I thought you said you'd tell me a joke, as in *one* joke."

"It would have been just one if you'd answered it right. Are you listening?"

Mara sighed again, as only one who was waiting to be queen could. "One more," she said, "then you're done."

"Okay. A turtle, a lion, a camel, a bear, a pig, a frog, two mice, and a snake all got under one tent. How many got wet?"

Mara pretended to think about her answer a long time before saying, "Nine."

Nathan rolled his eyes. "Wrong."

"How many, then?"

"None. It wasn't raining."

"That wasn't funny."

"*They* thought it was." Nathan pointed to the three children about them who were giggling.

"Their combined ages add up to eight. What do you expect?"

"Okay, I'll keep telling jokes until you find one you think is funny," Nathan said.

"Sorry, little brother, people don't live that long. But I will leave you with something funny just so you'll know what a real joke sounds like. Ready?"

"Go ahead."

"Knock, knock."

"Who's there?"

"Amana."

"Amana who?"

"Amana bad mood, so no more stupid jokes!"

As Mara got up to go over and talk with Karis, she saw Nathan point to her and heard him whisper to the little kids loud enough for her to hear, "When she's queen, she'll have to pay people to laugh at her lame jokes. But when I'm rabbi, people will write down everything I say!"

At first, Mara just slid down beside Karis and

said nothing. The minutes dragged on. Nathan soon ran out of jokes and the complaining started again.

"My leg hurts."

"My scarf is torn and I'll get in trouble."

"You *are* in trouble!"

"I'm *really* hungry now!"

"Why are we just sitting here doing nothing?"

"I want to look for my parents."

"No, we should stay put and let our parents find us."

"They sure won't look for us here."

"What's that in the corner? Is it a rat?"

The children whined for someone to do something. Akbar grabbed Obadiah's slingshot, loaded it with a small, hard bit of the crumbling wall, and started cautiously toward a small, dark shape in the far corner. Ten feet away, he suddenly leaped forward and landed on the shape, stomping on it twice for good measure. He reached down, picked it up, and waved it in the air. "One of Obadiah's sandals," he said disgustedly.

"Obie!" Mara scolded. "Why didn't you say so?"

Obadiah shrugged and grinned. "I was going to, but we had to see how Fearless Akbar the Hunter would save us from my sandal."

Akbar shot him a dirty look. Obadiah stuck out his hand for the slingshot. Akbar tossed it to him. "Let's get out of the city and hide in one of the villages," he said angrily. "I'm tired of this."

Sarah objected. "As long as we're right here, they don't know where we are."

Mara nodded. "I agree. It's probably still too dangerous to go out yet."

"But how will we know when it's safe to go out?" Sarah asked.

The whole time, Karis had kept her eyes closed and hadn't budged. But now she jumped to her feet and surprised Mara with a big smile. "I know how we'll find out."

"How?" asked Mara.

"We'll *spy!*"

W hat do you mean, 'we'?" Mara said. She wished for a small fire to dry her gown. She did *not* wish to go outside and spy.

"Suit yourself," said Karis with a shrug. "You're probably right. It would be better for you to stay here and baby-sit the little kids."

Mara ignored the remark. "And just what will *you* be doing?"

"I'll look for our parents and the other adults. I'll listen for the news in the market and bring back some food."

Obadiah shook his head. "You'll get caught and we'll be stuck underground wondering what happened to you."

Nathan cleared his throat and stood, hands folded in front of his chest. "The rabbis teach that when the Lord is with us, He will fight our battles. I say we let the Lord pound Saul good before we poke our heads out."

"Yeah, he's right for a change," Akbar said. "We should stick together until they give up looking for us."

Several of the others booed and said they'd rather be anywhere than where they were.

Sarah, who was usually quiet, said, "I don't know why we let Karis drag us down here. We should have listened to our mothers!" That drew several "yeahs" of agreement from the others, New Israel or not.

Mara was torn. Should she let Karis leave them in the strange, wet world under the city? Could she be trusted to come back for them after the way New Israel had treated her? She might even turn them in! No, that was silly. Their best chance was not sitting around getting on each other's nerves. They had to take action.

But the strongest thought Mara had was also the most unexpected. *What if Karis is caught spying and they hurt her?*

"I can't let you go alone," Mara said to everyone's surprise. "I'll go with you."

Karis stared at her. "Really? It'd be safer to work

together, that's for sure." She paused. "Thanks," she said at last.

They spent the next few minutes collecting coins from the kids for food. As usual, Karis had no coins to contribute.

"You never have any money," Mara said. "Can't your dad juggle or sing or do anything for spare change? He should stop sponging off the church, you know. I've seen monkeys at the market that earn more than he does!"

Mara bit the inside of her cheek. She was irritated that she cared if Karis got caught, so she let the hateful words tumble out. But she did manage to stop the other mean words she had in mind.

Instantly, the friendliness in Karis's eyes disappeared and Mara felt horrible. She didn't like that feeling, so she turned her attention to the others and tried reassuring them that this was the best plan. "Just two of us looking will draw a lot less attention than all of us running around," said Mara.

The others grumbled and Mara started to sing, "We are New Israel . . ." With little enthusiasm, the other club members halfheartedly finished the last two lines.

Karis frowned. "We've got to come up with

some new words for that song. Something for everyone, and definitely more praise, less brag." She smiled a little. Reluctantly, Mara smiled too.

The girls said their good-byes, left Obadiah and Akbar in charge, and dropped to the ground to wiggle out of the room the way they'd wiggled in. Nathan dropped down beside his sister.

"What do you think you're doing?" Mara questioned.

"Going with you," Nathan said. "The rabbis teach that a cord of three strands is not quickly broken. I make three, and that's stronger than two." He waited until Karis was through to the other side before speaking low in Mara's ear. "Can we trust her? You need me. The queen always needs a bodyguard."

Mara looked at her brother's skinny body. It would be another 10 years before he sprouted any muscles. Still, she figured it would be nice to have him around. "Okay," she said. "But no more jokes. I mean it!"

"Yes, your royal bossiness!"

Out of the room they crawled, with only the faithful little lamp—now re-lit—for light. After the bright torches, the tunnel seemed pitch-black again, despite the tiny spot of lamplight.

Karis stood nose to nose with Nathan, the unexpected third party. Her face was half shadowed, half lit, eye sockets dark and empty like a skull's. But way back in there, a small spark in each eye said he'd better not cause any problems. "Stay close," she said before starting back at a trot along the passage the way they'd come.

It took the trio far less time to wind back to the paving stone entrance than it had to herd all the children to the abandoned water well. Mara saw that Karis must have arranged the paving stones back in place to cover their escape. Now Karis listened for sounds of someone moving around above. Apparently hearing none, she shoved the stones away, took a fast look around, then motioned Mara and Nathan to follow.

Quickly, they darted back to the central business district, their clothes drying in the warm late-afternoon air, then melted into the crowd shopping for plums and cloth and live chickens. Vendors called to the shoppers, each trying to make a sale.

"Fresh, nice fish pulled from the Sea of Galilee!"

"Beautiful fabrics the color of the sky!"

"Fine white wool of the highest quality!"

A donkey caravan clanked up the street of metal-workers, hammered brass utensils glinting in the sun.

Coming close to the wine vendor's stall, the three kids overheard a heated exchange of news.

"Another dozen believers in the Way were arrested but an hour ago!" said a large, red-faced man with a wheeze. "Add them to those taken in this morning's raid at the ringleader Joshua's house, and we'll be paying taxes for a new jail to hold them all. Of course, they shouted that they have hurt no one, but we all know the strange ideas they spread. The Way, indeed! The way to ruin, I say!"

"That's nothing!" said a thick barrel of a man, tugging down the sleeves of a dirty gray cloak that was much too small for him. "Saul broke into the nut vendor's cellar and found 20 or more of them praying beneath the floorboards! If they have nothing to hide, how come that's where you usually find them?"

"Jail them all!" sputtered the owner of the wine stall. "They buy little from me. Instead, they raise much of their own food and share it with one another. Why? Isn't our meat and drink good enough for them?"

The donkey caravan clattered by, the little animals looking hot and tired and in need of a cool drink.

From across the street came the angry shouts and threats of a terrible argument. A throng of people spilled into the street, yelling and pointing. The donkeys stopped in their tracks and the kids dropped to their knees in the dusty street, using the animals to shield them from view.

They peered between the bony legs of the beasts at the realization of their worst fears. Saul, grim-faced and determined, was crossing the street flanked by armed police. He was coming straight toward them.

Just then, a beautiful woman in silky yellow grabbed Saul by the arm and tried to stop him. Roughly, he shoved her away. She stumbled and fell to her knees but was instantly up and pulling on Saul's arm and beating against him with her fists. Others swarmed noisily about them like irritated hornets and in turn were hit and pushed by the men at Saul's side.

"My husband!" the woman screamed in Aramaic. "Where is my husband? Where have you taken him?"

"What's she saying?" Karis asked. Mara told her.

Two big men with sweat-smeared faces grabbed the woman's arms and pulled her back. Saul threw her a chilling look of disgust and moved on.

"Your husband trusts in this Jesus Messiah, and he must pay for the false beliefs he teaches to others!" another woman shouted. "They will track down as many 'believers' as they can get their hands on!"

"Murderer!" the woman in yellow screamed at Saul's back.

Mara peeked around the hind legs of a sleepy-eyed donkey with enormous ears, hoping for a better view. She saw the awful hatred in Saul's reddened eyes. It was the look of evil.

And suddenly those evil eyes seemed to look right at her.

"Hyah! Move, you miserable creatures! Hyah!" The donkey driver whacked the rear donkey across the rump with a switch and the caravan lurched forward.

The kids scrambled to their feet, and crouching over so as not to be seen from the other side, they kept step with the caravan until they could hide behind a pile of fruit sacks.

"Phew!" Karis exclaimed. "That was close!"

"Did you see his eyes?" Mara said shakily. "Maybe Saul's the monster everybody says lives in the tunnels!"

They both looked at Nathan, who was as pale as parchment. Without taking his eyes off Saul and his thugs, he muttered, "Did you see what I saw?"

"Of course we did," said Mara. "We were right there with you."

"No, no, you were too busy watching the argument. Didn't you see what Saul and his men had on them?"

The girls gave Nathan a quizzical look. "What?" they said in unison.

"B-blood," Nathan stammered.

The three gulped as one.

"Let's go," Karis ordered.

"Yes," said Nathan. "Suddenly, those tunnels don't seem so bad."

"Not the tunnels," said Karis. "This way." She set off in the direction Saul and his men had gone.

Mara stopped her. "What do you think you're doing?"

"Yeah," agreed Nathan. "What do you think you're doing?"

Karis rolled her eyes. "Is there an echo out here? We've got to follow them and find out what they're up to. The last time we saw our parents, Saul had them!"

"Good point," Mara said.

"This is stupid," Nathan said. "Why don't we just have Saul over to the house for supper? After dessert, we'll ask him if he wouldn't please take us to our parents."

"Your brother's got a mouth," Karis said.

"You should hear him when he's in a bad mood," Mara replied.

The girls smiled at each other. Nathan shook his head. "Queen, you make a bodyguard's job very difficult."

Mara patted him on the head. "I meant to thank you for guarding me from the big, bad donkeys."

Nathan started to stick his tongue out, but must have thought better of it.

The trio crept after the men. Saul led his band into the stall of Porteous the potter. In front of the stall, beautiful horses the color of fine black tea were tied to iron rings set in a horizontal post. Two of the men checked on the horses before following Saul and the others beneath a shady awning.

"Thank you, Porteous, for watching the horses while we checked the area for fugitives. Those 'believers' would hide in a camel's nose if they could find a way in."

His friends laughed with him. All except Saul, whose face was like a dark thundercloud. They sat on upturned water pots and began to discuss the coming evening's activities. Porteous, in white turban and expensive green cloak, looked nervous at having them there. They were rough and dirty men and looked like they wrestled lions in their spare time. And their garments *were* streaked with blood.

"How are we going to get close enough to hear what they're saying?" asked Mara uneasily.

Karis looked around. "There. He'll help us."

"He" was the water vendor, working his way along the street with two large goatskins on his belt and an impossibly large water urn balanced on his head. "Ho, you thirsty ones, come and drink!" he cried. An occasional customer would stop the man and pay him for a cup of fresh springwater.

The men ignored the water man. But just as he came even with the stall of Porteous, the children ran up and paid for drinks with a few of the coins they had collected from the others underground.

The man stood in the shade cast by the huge, carefully balanced water urn and cheerfully filled three metal cups. He waited for the children to finish.

They took their time. A very long time. And while their mouths sipped the cool water, their ears strained to catch every word of the men loudly talking a few feet behind them.

"We've got to wipe these 'believers' out," said one. "There are too many of them; they're upsetting our religious leaders."

Mara snuck a peek at the men.

"And when the religious leaders become upset, we all become upset," said a particularly burly man with a jagged scar from one ear to the point of his chin.

"Few will miss them," a third man offered. "It's not like they hold important offices or contribute much to the economy. Many of them are old and some are women."

Mara shivered despite the midday sun. *If women and old people aren't important to Saul,* she thought, *then children must not be very valuable either. Why doesn't Saul say something?*

"I told you we shouldn't have let those people go this morning," accused the man with the scar. "You can frighten them, but it only seems to make them stronger and more determined. We should have killed them while we could!"

Nathan choked on his water, and Mara and Karis both pounded his back. "Our parents," he squeaked, "they're free! We can go home!"

Mara and Karis laughed loudly to cover Nathan's words. Mara peeked under her arm again. Saul sat still as stone, his eyes burning with a fanatical light.

"Here's what we do," came the voice of the first man, looking annoyed at the noisy children in front of the potter's stall. "We must rid Jerusalem of these unwelcome people and stop this foolish faith in that crucified Jesus before it has a chance to grow by even one more person."

"When?"

"Tonight. My friends tell me the church of the Way plans a meeting at the same house we were at this morning. The fools think we won't raid the same place twice. There they'll be, giving thanks that we didn't keep them in prison after all. We take a hundred armed men and we storm that meeting. This time, we finish the job."

Nathan choked again. The girls pounded him again.

"Are you done, children?" cried the water vendor impatiently. "I have other customers waiting. Do you wish more water? No? Then your cups, please. Give me your cups."

The man with the scar startled them. "What's the matter here? Vendor, do you not see we're trying to have a discussion? Move along and take these—"

He stopped and peered at Karis, nearest him, who was pulling her hair across her face. "Hey, weren't you at that meeting of the Way this morning?"

Mara and Nathan edged away, averting their faces.

The water man repositioned his huge water urn and hastily moved off. Mara and Nathan stayed ahead of him in the shadow cast by nine feet of man and jar. He shooed them off.

Karis stayed right where she was, the shoulder of her threadbare gown tight in the grip of the scar-faced man. "Yes, you were there!" he shouted eagerly. "You and those other kids slipped out before we could catch you!"

Safely away from Saul's company, Mara and Nathan looked back.

Nathan laughed dryly. "She doesn't look so sure of herself now that she's about to get what's coming to her!"

Mara stopped and just about lifted Nathan out of his sandals. "No!" she snapped, giving him a good shake. "Do you remember what our father said at the meeting this morning when everyone was ready to fight each other? He said, 'Would Jesus be pleased with us?' Would He, Nathan? Would Jesus want us to let those men hurt Karis?"

Mara surprised herself. Was she changing her mind about Karis? She couldn't stop thinking about the rocks raining down on poor Stephen. She wouldn't want the same thing to happen to Karis.

Nathan's eyes dropped and he shook his head. "Nawh," he said, shamefaced. "He wouldn't want that."

"Then you'd better ask God to make you invisible, because we're going back there!"

Nathan tried to give her a look like she'd lost her mind, but she was already 12 steps ahead of him.

They hurried back the way they'd come, hidden behind a large cart piled high with baskets of every size and shape. When the cart drew abreast of the potter's stall, Mara and Nathan dropped to a crouch so that they could not be seen. Large decorative clay pots blocked them from the view of the men who were still shouting at Karis and paying no attention to the street.

"Where are the other children? Tell us!"

"You're not from Jerusalem, are you? Where are you from?"

"You'd better loosen your little Greek tongue or we'll loosen it for you."

"Take a good look at the setting sun, my girl, because you won't be seeing it again for a very long time!"

Mara and Nathan scurried quietly between the horses that were tied to the post, then turned and faced the tall animals. Mara reached up and untied the reins of the horses nearest her, and Nathan followed suit with those nearest him.

At first the animals only shuffled their feet and nickered softly, uncertain of what was happening. Mara looked at Nathan and he nodded. On the silent count of three, they jerked upright, flapped their arms, and screeched like crazed owls.

With a wild whinnying, the horses stampeded.

Ears flattened, snorting madly, they whirled and bucked and kicked away down the street in opposite directions, nearly taking Porteous' awning with them.

The stunned men chased after their horses, forgetting Karis, who had twisted out of the big man's grasp. They ran, yelling terrible curses and threats at anything that moved. Saul's rage was the worst. He swore to put an end to the Way. He would not rest until he had killed them all.

Mara, Karis, and Nathan ran for their lives. Back to the tunnel entrance they flew. Suddenly, the terrifying underground passage looked like one of the safest places on earth.

CHAPTER 8

Did you see the look on that big horse when I jumped up in his face?" Nathan was bent over, partly from lack of breath, partly from laughing so hard.

"Just like nearsighted Aunt Isabel looked the time she asked for the hairbrush and you handed her a lizard," Mara gasped, trying to gain back her own wind.

"Yeah," Karis said, "but it was no worse than the look on my face when I saw you two sneaking away with the water vendor. I actually thought you were going to leave me with those goons!"

Nathan stopped laughing. He couldn't look either girl in the eye. Mara took a sudden interest in her fingernails.

"Oh, great!" Karis huffed. "You *were* going to leave me there!"

"Not Mara, just me," Nathan mumbled. "And

I . . . well, I wasn't thinking very clearly." His face reddened with shame. "Sorry."

"*You're* sorry? So am I!" Karis yelled. "Here I risk my neck to help New Israel to safety, and the minute you have the chance, you feed me to the hyenas. Is that what Torah teaches?"

"No." Nathan looked miserable. "Go ahead. I deserve it. You won't tell the rabbis, will you?"

Karis looked ready to blast him with a few more choice complaints, but she clamped her mouth shut instead. She shook her head and started off at a trot. "It's getting late. We've got to hurry."

They headed for the tunnels and the secret hideout where the others waited.

Mara hurried to catch up with Karis's flying feet. She felt all funny inside, like she'd swallowed a pound of squirming caterpillars and they weren't planning to stay down. Karis had every right to be mad. They hadn't treated her well at all. Once they were safe again, Mara would have to think of some way to make it up to her. Good queens made sure of things like that.

After several twists, turns, and shortcuts through the city, they were once again in the alley with the removable paving stones.

Mara couldn't believe it. Karis was pulling at the stones and singing the New Israel song. At least it was the club tune; as Mara drew close, it was obvious they were not the club words:

"We are New Israel, kids who fuss and fight;
People avoid us 'cause we kick and bite!
About your bad kids, we hurt feelings left and
    right.
We think we're good, but we're just rude
And offend everyone in sight!"

Mara helped her push the stones aside. "You've got too many syllables in the last line," she said. "And 'good' and 'rude' don't rhyme so well."

Karis looked at her. Mara smiled weakly.

At last Karis smiled too. "Songwriting is hard work," she said. "It takes a long time to get something worth singing."

Mara let it go.

Once they'd wiggled their way back into the secret hideout, Mara, Nathan, and Karis were pelted with questions from the other kids.

"What took you so long?"

"Are our parents okay?"

"Can we go now?"

"What did you bring us back to eat?"

The last question was perhaps the most difficult to answer. Everyone talked at the same time and it was hard to get the story out.

Mara tried. "We spent the food money on water."

"Water! But we're hungry!"

"It was too dangerous to buy food once they recognized us. Besides, we didn't have time; we had to scare the horses."

"Horses? What horses?"

"Did she say she bought us horses to eat?"

"Not to eat! We spooked the horses to run from the owners who were holding Karis . . ."

"My tummy's howling," Obadiah's little sister cried.

Obadiah gave her a hug. "No, Rebecca, you mean your stomach is growling."

She patted her round belly. "No, 'diah," she insisted. "Listen. It's howling!"

Akbar took off a sandal and stared at it. "This is starting to look tastier by the minute."

"We can eat later. Right now, we've got to do something and do it fast," Mara said, taking charge. "It'll be dark soon and our parents will be worried sick about us. Their lives are in danger. We've got to go back, find them, and tell them to get out of Jerusalem as fast as they can. If Saul and his men find them gathered at my house, there's no telling what they'll do."

Actually, she could imagine exactly what they'd do, but Mara wasn't about to tell the little ones. The worry in the eyes of the older kids told her they also knew what Saul the executioner would do to their families.

By the time they got it all sorted out, everyone was grumpier and hungrier than ever. But they had a plan.

They wormed their way out through the well entrance and froze. Far down the passageway, in the direction the chalk arrow pointed, the flickering of flames was reflected off the tunnel walls. Voices. Distant shouts. The trampling of feet on stone. Saul's men were coming!

"Quickly!" Karis hissed. "Hold hands and walk swiftly. We can move faster than they can."

Single file, hands tightly holding hands, the children made their way back to the spot where they had entered the wet world beneath Jerusalem.

Obadiah and Akbar got on their hands and knees to form a step up. Mara helped the children onto the big boys' backs, and Karis reached down a hand and pulled them up and out onto the street.

Halfway through this operation, Karis called down. "Wait! Someone's coming. Not a sound!"

She plugged the hole haphazardly with the paving stones and sat down on them with two children on her lap. Her legs blocked the place in the pavement from which several children had just emerged.

Mara gulped as the way of escape was shut off. Faint echoes from behind grew louder. Then stopped.

"Here!" The word was clear and angry.

"Hurry! Stop them now!" This was followed by sounds of splashing. Saul's men were closing in!

"... and the goat and the rooster decided to travel to Judea all by themselves." Mara could hear Karis talking loudly, as if telling the others a story. "So the goat says to the rooster, 'Do you think that if I crowed to the rising sun every morning I would grow beautiful red feathers just like yours?' 'Well,' said the rooster, ruffling his shiny coat of fine red feathers, 'I suppose that will happen just as soon as I'm able to grow horns by butting the farmer every time he bends over...'"

There must be strangers nearby aboveground, too! Mara felt caught between two jaws of a trap about to slam shut. She couldn't go back; she couldn't go forward. She prayed, *God, please save us!*

Sudden dim light. Hands reaching down. Pulling. The danger above had passed and Karis was pulling them out. They were free!

When all were finally out, Akbar and Obadiah included, the bigger kids forced the stones back into place.

"Nobody . . . will . . . be . . . any . . . the . . . wiser," puffed Obadiah, giving each of the stones a couple of last mighty shoves. The first one fit snug as could be, but the second stone was slightly smaller than the opening. With the large boy's encouragement, it went right on through and fell into the stream at the bottom of the tunnel with a disheartening splash-thud.

"Oops!" Obadiah said. The others stared at him in disgust and fear.

"Obie, you're a real menace to society sometimes," said Akbar.

"Listen!" Karis commanded. "Voices from below! They're here!"

The children ran as if their feet had sprouted wings.

"Split up!" Mara yelled when they reached the business district. "That'll make it harder for them to chase us. Obie, you and Akbar each take a group. Karis, you and Sarah take another. The rest of you, come with me and Nathan. We'll meet at my house. Quick now, go!"

They went, darting under carts, dodging through crowds, leaping over beggars, and racing to warn the believers as if the devil were at their backs. Mara believed he was—and Saul was his name.

All the kids reached Mara's house at about the same time and were set to burst in on the gathering, except for one thing. A 300-pound man blocked the door.

"Whoa! Why are you kids in such a big hurry? The meeting's already begun," said the man with a shake of his hairy head. "You don't get inside unless you've got a note from Caesar himself!"

"Benjamin!" cried Mara, throwing her arms partway around the man's tree-trunk-sized waist. "Are we ever glad to see you!"

Benjamin's eyes widened in surprise. "Miss Mara! Nathan! You're all here! I didn't recognize you, all soggy and dirty like that. We've been worried sick about you. Your parents are inside . . ."

"Not for long," replied Mara grimly. "Saul is on his way. Quick, let us in!"

Benjamin practically took the door from its hinges. The kids tumbled into the room amid cries of disbelief and joy from the adults crowding the room. Mara's father, who had been on his knees leading the church in prayer, leaped to his feet and hugged Mara and Nathan until she thought their bones would crack.

"Friends! Believers! Rejoice!" Joshua shouted to be heard. "Our prayers are answered! Let's sing a hymn of thanks to God for the safe return—"

"No, Father!" Before people could recover from their shock at her behavior, Mara climbed onto the eating table that had been shoved to one side of the room. That produced another gasp from the crowd. But there she stood, back straight, knees rattling like dried beans in a bowl. "Forgive me, but we don't have time to sing. Saul and his men are close by. They're coming to destroy our meeting. They're coming to destroy *us*. We've got to escape!"

Fear froze everyone as still as statues. From outside, shouts and running footsteps grew steadily louder.

Benjamin opened the door a crack to peer out, then slammed it shut. He turned, planted huge feet against the floor, and braced his broad back against the oncoming attack. "They have swords and knives," he announced. "There are 50 or 60 or more."

"This way to the courtyard," shouted Joshua, indicating the back of the house. "We must go out the gate or scramble over the wall and scatter in every direction. It is our only hope. Find the best way out of the city that you can. If God wills, we will meet again one day—if not on earth, then in heaven. Hurry now! Don't look back!"

The mob reached the door and, with blood-curdling yells and curses, threw their weight against it. Benjamin strained to shove them back, his great shaggy head a sweaty tangle. With a startling bang, something heavy and solid bashed against the door, wood on wood.

"Battering ram!" grunted Benjamin. "Can't hold them much longer!"

But when Joshua moved to help him, Benjamin growled, "No, friend, no! Take your wife and young ones and run! Old Benjamin will see what our neighbors have in mind. *Run!*"

They ran, Joshua with an arm around his wife, and Mara and Nathan right on their heels. Other New Israel kids and their parents, and some of Karis's friends and their families, fled with them.

Past the shrubs and flowers that were Mara's mother's pride and joy. Past the pretty little olive tree that Mara had planted and watered day after day. Past the small brick well that Nathan and Joshua had proudly built together, brick by brick.

Night was falling, a large harvest moon lighting their way.

"Where can we go?" moaned Mara's mother. "Our whole lives are here."

"Hurry!" urged Joshua, motioning them out the gate. "We have money. We can buy passage somewhere."

Loud, angry voices sounded from inside the house. Benjamin bellowed like a wild bull. Something tipped over and landed with a crash.

Behind them, Karis's mother stumbled and fell, catching the dangling ties of her cloak in the gate. Timon, her husband, yanked frantically to free her, but the more he pulled, the tighter the cords became entangled.

"Take it off!" gasped Timon. "Hurry!"

Terrible screams sounded from the house. Karis's eyes darted from the house to her parents struggling to get the cloak off to Mara up ahead. "Help us!" the eyes pleaded. "Don't leave our family here to die!"

Mara reached toward her. "Karis, give me your hand. We can't wait for anything. Run!"

But Karis shrank back, not sure what to do.

"Karis, go with Mara," Timon shouted. "We'll catch up!"

More bloodcurdling screams. Karis covered her ears, eyes squeezed shut, and did not move. She was frozen to the spot with fear.

"Mara!" her father shouted, holding the gate open for his daughter. "Come on! There's nothing else we can do here!"

Mara started after him. *If it weren't for Karis, New Israel would be in the Jerusalem jail.* Mara stopped. *She stuck her neck out and kept you safe even after you treated her like sewer slop.* The thoughts were like daggers stabbing at her brain.

"Father!" Mara called. "My friend and her parents need help. Can we take them, please?"

"Bring them!" Joshua ordered. "This way! Hurry!"

Mara ran back and helped Timon pull the cloak away and untangle his wife. Mara grabbed Karis's hand and pulled. "Come! Now!"

The two families ran for their lives. Whenever someone dropped back from fatigue, the others pulled and carried the tired one along. Saul had sworn to kill every believer. If they hesitated, Jerusalem would be their grave.

Mara and Karis led the group down the less-traveled side streets with which they were becoming increasingly familiar. After 10 minutes of this, they were within sight of the western gate of the city.

It was swarming with soldiers and citizens armed with clubs. Torch flames danced like orange demons, turning the shadows of the men into Goliaths against the high stone walls. The fugitives couldn't tell exactly what was being said, but the tone of the voices left no doubt that all of Jerusalem was on the alert for runaway believers.

It did not appear that they had been followed. The families crouched inside the toolshed of a wheelwright who was a believer. But he was nowhere around and the shop was eerily silent. The walls flickered with distant torchlight. Both sets of parents discussed their predicament for a while but were unable to find a solution.

Then Joshua turned and spoke low to the children. There was no mistaking the concern in his voice. "This means all routes out of the city are blocked," he said.

"Not all," said Karis.

"Don't be silly, girl," said Joshua. "Anyone can see we're trapped."

"Anyone but God," Mara said, smiling at Karis. "He's given our underground sister here a special talent."

Karis's mom looked questioningly at Karis's dad.

Joshua looked sharply at his daughter. Her mother frowned. "Mara, this is no time for make-believe."

Nathan adjusted his turban and placed his hands together like a priest. "Better listen to her, Dad. Torah speaks of gaining wisdom. Um, recent experience has taught me that it may be possible for even a female to do so." He looked embarrassed. "Mara knows a lot for a girl," he finished in a mumble.

Nathan's mother looked at him in amazement. "Are you feeling all right?"

Mara looked at him with suspicion. "Think. At any time were you kicked in the head by a horse today?"

Karis put her arm around Mara. "Nathan was just stating a fact. Mara does know a lot." She grinned. "Now, if you'll all just please follow us . . ."

CHAPTER 9

W hoa, there," Nathan interrupted. "What about those muscle men of Saul's that nearly grabbed our tails before we got out of the tunnels? They may still be down there, ready to toss our turbans the minute we come down."

Karis shook her head. "That's what you think. Aren't you taught many ways to tunnel into Torah? There are also many ways to enter and leave the underground tunnels of Hezekiah. I know one way it would take the brains of a thousand kings to figure out. Follow me!"

"One minute," Joshua said. "We need more light."

He walked toward a group vigorously arguing over which way to go in search of Jesus' followers. "A torch, my good man?" he said loudly to a young fellow with two. "A person needs all the light he can gather to spot something so slippery and low to the ground as a 'believer'!" The young man laughed and tossed Joshua a torch before settling on a direction in which to continue the hunt.

Joshua waited for the rest of the mob to follow the young man, then hurried back to the shed, much to the relief of the others.

They wound down a dozen different streets and alleys, sometimes waiting long, anxious minutes in hiding for a noisy crowd or troop of soldiers to pass before continuing. In those moments of waiting, many prayers were whispered and the children received reassuring hugs by their parents. When danger passed, they hurried again after Karis, guided by the moon, their torch, and their strong faith.

An hour later they turned the corner of a low stone fence and entered a deserted courtyard close by the city wall. In the middle stood a decaying stone well. Karis stopped at the well, leaned over, and started untying the frayed rope that ended in a bucket made of animal skins.

"Good," said Nathan wearily. "Now that you've taken us by the scenic route, I could use a drink."

"Wait until we're down," Karis replied, freeing the bucket and giving the thick rope several tugs.

After a few seconds, the wheel that raised and lowered the bucket turned easily.

"D-d-down?" Nathan faltered. "What do you mean 'down'? What do you mean 'we'?"

"I mean that at the bottom of this dry rain well is a break in the wall eventually leading to the main water system where we were this afternoon. Saul doesn't have enough men to guard every tunnel and entrance. They'll be looking for us where they heard us last, not way back here in a bunch of passages nobody uses anymore. Ladies first?"

Mara and her family looked dubiously at the flimsy bucket of sewn camel hide.

Karis's father saw their hesitation and spoke. "I know my daughter. If she says it's safe, we can trust that it's safe."

Karis's mother pulled her daughter close and nodded. "My husband is right," she said. "And the longer we stand here in the moonlight, torch blazing, the greater the chance someone will come to investigate."

Realizing the truth of that statement, both families lined up for the ride down the well. The men first lowered the mothers, then the daughters, and then Nathan by way of the rope and bucket. Joshua insisted on being last and lowered Karis's father next.

It was about 20 feet to the bottom, where Karis had long ago spread a large quantity of sour hay that a stabler had discarded behind his stalls. She had thrown it down the well, then come in by a different entrance to spread it out on the floor below. Several layers later, she had herself a semisoft landing.

Joshua, the last, tied the bucket as low as possible, then climbed down and hung from it, subtracting a good eight feet from his fall. He focused on the light of the torch below, said a prayer, and let go.

The landing was not a graceful one, but with no bones broken, they all thanked God and scrambled through a low, narrow opening into a passage where they could stand. Mara missed the friendly moonlight the minute it was gone.

Karis looked in one direction, then the other. But she was taking too long. Mara could see Karis hesitate. She was unsure.

The weight of the world above pressed down upon them. Fury, hatred, swords, knives . . .

"This way!" Karis finally declared. "Quickly!"

For what seemed like hours, they wound

through narrow places. The subterranean chill crept into their bones and left them shivering. Sometimes the stone floor was slick and the footing difficult. Mara worried about someone turning an ankle that would slow them down and make them easier for Saul to find. She worried about her skinny brother, especially when he stumbled into her and she could feel his body shaking with cold and fright.

If anything were to happen to Karis, Mara wondered how they would ever find their way to the surface.

But at least here in these caverns the water did not flow. The dry season had lessened the amount of water coming in from the springs in the valley of Kidron, and this lessening seemed to keep the water channeled into the main tunnel.

Mara worried about why they had not yet reached the main tunnel. She forced her mind away from the one word that made her eyes well with tears: *Lost*.

Karis stopped. Mara and the others stopped too, their rapid breathing the only sound in the barren passageway.

"Wait here." Karis ran ahead with the torch, plunging the others into utter darkness. Mara could hear the girl's footsteps scraping against the hard rock floor ahead, her breathing growing more ragged with each step.

Something was wrong.

"Cave-in," Karis called out. The word sent a stab of cold right through Mara's heart. They'd have to go back. But they could not climb up the sheer sides of the well. Was there another way out?

As if in answer, angry voices sounded from another direction. Saul's men! Coming closer. *That must be the way to the main chamber, but we can't use it now! They're coming. We've got to get away!*

Karis appeared, her face grim in the torchlight. She would not look at Mara—or anyone else. "I was sure that was the way past the main channel, but it's completely blocked," she said faintly. "I thought there was a way around it, but—but I can't find it. We'll have to go back to the well. Th-there might be enough loose stones for us to make a pile to stand on so that our dads can grab the bucket. Hurry! At least maybe we can hide in the ha—"

She turned abruptly and started along a passage Mara didn't remember at all.

"Wait. That's not the way we came." Mara felt panicky and was about to use the word she knew they were all thinking. *Lost. Admit it. L-O-S-T. We should never have—*

The floor beneath their feet began to shake and roll. From deep within the earth came a low rumble. Karis jumped back and knocked into Mara and Nathan. All fell in a heap just as the ceiling ahead let go with a deafening roar and filled the passage where Karis had been, as well as the one Mara thought was the right one, with tons of earth and rubble.

Earthquake!

The torch rolled away into a patch of water and sputtered out. They lay on their backs against the cold stone floor, stunned by the collapse and the clouds of dust that swirled into their eyes and lungs and left them choking for air.

Mara felt confused. *The torch went out. How come we can still see?*

Shouts again, closer this time. The sound of running feet. Saul coming. Mara prayed, *God, don't let us die like this! Open the earth and pull us out!*

"Look!" Karis cried, pointing upward. The dust was clearing and a shaft of light—bright, silvery moonlight—streamed down through a hole in the ground above made by the fresh cave-in.

"Swiftly!" ordered Joshua. "Children, you first. Climb toward that light with everything you've got. Go!"

Joshua didn't need to say another word. Saul's men did it for him. "This way!" came the clear shouts, now fearfully close.

Karis, Mara, and Nathan clawed and pulled their way upward. Dirt and rock showered down on their parents below, but it didn't stop the adults from scrambling up after them. Sweet, warm air met them at the top, along with a wonderful surprise. They were outside the city walls!

"Messiah has saved us!" Joshua declared.

"Amen!" Nathan yelped.

Timon threw his arms wide to the sky. "Praise God!" he cried.

The seven fugitives grabbed each other's hands and ran like the wind in the direction of Caesarea. They ran until they looked back and saw no sign of any torches. Nothing but darkness and the bright moon.

Mara's panting slowed and she gave her brother a giant hug, then the same for each of her parents. Head down, she went to Karis. "What I said earlier about your father and earning money, it—it was a stupid thing to say. I've said a lot of stupid things. I'm sorry for making you feel bad about little stuff that isn't important at all. I believe in Jesus and so do you. And back there when we escaped the house? I was just as scared as you were!"

Karis gave her a big smile. "Does this mean I'm good enough to be in New Israel?"

Mara looked at Nathan, who nodded, then frowned. "Except compared to the way we acted, she might be too good for the club!" he said.

Mara smiled. "No, we're done with that. Besides, wherever we end up, we'll have to start another club. Let's call it *Brand*-New Israel!"

Nathan groaned.

Karis rolled her eyes.

CHAPTER 10

"P lease pass the goat cheese," Nathan said, wiping his mouth on the sleeve of a rough cotton cloak that easily had room inside for another boy and a half. But it was warm, clean, and dry. Nathan hungrily helped himself to a hunk of cheese as thick as a man's hand.

"We may have escaped with little more than the clothes on our backs," Joshua was saying, "but here we have found a king's treasure in brotherly love and concern. Christ be with this house!"

The seven who had escaped underground from Jerusalem had traveled three more days to reach Judea's major seaport of Caesarea. At first they attempted to stay off the roads as much as possible, but on the second day Joshua paid for a ride the rest of the way in the smelly wagon of a cheerful fish merchant returning to his catch on the Mediterranean Sea.

The fisherman said nothing about the troubles in Jerusalem. If he suspected that his four adult and three child passengers were running away from something, he did not say so. In fact, he spent most of the journey whistling lively tunes that Mara figured could easily charm fish into the man's boat. Who needed a net? Before they reached Caesarea, the kind whistler had offered both Timon and Joshua jobs mending nets and drying fish.

The footsore travelers had arrived at the home of Azariah Bar-jona, Timon's brother. Azariah owned a clothing stall that sold beautiful woolen fabrics woven by his wife, Ruth, and two neighbor women who worked for her. There was a new baby in the house and three other small children.

Now all 13 people were gathered around a table that the Bar-jona brothers had quickly built of wooden planking from an old rowboat falling to pieces behind the house.

Mara smiled at Karis, who smiled back. "I think what I've been missing all along is a sister," said Mara.

"Me, too," said Karis, giving Mara's hand a squeeze.

"Hey!" protested Nathan around a mouthful of cheese. "I thought I was all the sibling you ever needed!"

Mara winked at Karis. "No, brother, you'll be much too busy polishing my crown and scepter. The queen needs a sister."

"For what?" Nathan bit into a thick slice of fresh-baked bread and butter.

"Lots of things," Mara replied with a sniff. "To go shopping with. To do each other's hair." She looked at the straight black hair on Karis's head and vowed to fix it. At least the tangled knot was gone. After a nice hot bath, they all looked and smelled better. "And to order you around when I'm too busy feeding the peacocks and bathing in milk," Mara finished. She shared a grin with Karis.

"Yuck!" Nathan's face twisted as if his mouth were full of something sour. "I'd rather be sprinkled with maggot spit and buried in eel slime!"

"Such a gentleman," Mara said with a laugh. "My hero!" She leaned over and kissed him.

"Knock it off!" he yelped, rubbing frantically at his cheek. "Torah does not encourage public displays of affection. You really must learn proper manners . . ."

"Thank you, Rabbi Maggot Spit. I'll try to remember that."

Mara's mother shook her head and frowned, but everyone else laughed. Karis leaned across Nathan and whispered in Mara's ear. "There's another thing a sister's good for."

"What?" Mara whispered back.

"Exploring. Caesarea has tons of marble and lots of hiding places around the harbor. And best of all, there's a six-mile-long tunnel cut through Mount Carmel to bring water into the city from underground springs. I'll show it to you!"

Mara rolled her eyes. "No way! At least not right now. Give it a rest for a few days and we'll see."

The two girls giggled and Nathan showed them the ugly wad of goat cheese in his mouth.

But soon all were giving thanks for each other and for how God had brought the three families together as friends.

Joshua asked, "Is Jesus pleased when we argue over whether we worship the heavenly Father in Greek ways or Hebrew ways?"

"No!" the others answered in unison. Even the littlest ones, though their "nos" were late, joined in the fun. Only the wide-eyed baby kept silent.

"Does Jesus say Hebrew customs are better than Greek customs?"

"No!"

"Does Jesus love both those who speak Greek and those who speak Aramaic?"

Several of the smaller children, sure of the right answer this time, answered with a loud "no!" as the adults were answering with a resounding "yes!" Mara laughed at the sheepish looks on their faces.

"Are all of us who follow the Way of Christ really brothers and sisters in Christ?"

"Yes! Yes! Yes!"

Timon reached for his wife's hand. She reached for Joshua's hand just as his hand took hold of Mara's. Mara grabbed Nathan's hand before it could get away, and he shyly placed his other hand in Karis's. When the circle of hands was complete, Azariah prayed: "Merciful Father, thank You for forgiving our foolishness and protecting us from evil. Thank You for bringing the ones we love and the ones we have come to love safe from the dangers of Jerusalem. Bless the believers still there and keep them from harm. But should they die for their faith, Father, please give them a place in heaven with You and Stephen. Make the church grow, Lord, and may it spread across the Roman Empire and beyond. In the strong name of Jesus the Messiah, we pray."

Mara asked if she could add a prayer. Nathan started to say, "The rabbis do not permit a woman to lead prayer in pub—" but Azariah cut him off.

"Of course you may pray, Mara. Jesus would stop no one from talking to the Father."

Mara bowed her head and tried not to cry. "Father God, please watch over Sarah and Obadiah and Akbar and the other kids and their families. Please let us see them again someday. Thank You for Stephen and his faith in You. And I ask You to change Saul's heart. Help him to trust in Jesus. And thank You for changing my heart so—so—I mean, forgive me for the way I treated Karis. Bless her family for giving us a place to stay. Help me to be a nicer person. In the name of Jesus."

"Amen!" Nathan said with too much enthusiasm. Mara poked him with her elbow.

"Lord"—Karis's voice was soft and could barely be heard—"please forgive me for thinking every kid in New Israel has dirt for brains."

"A-double-men!" Nathan said, earning himself another elbow.

———————

The three friends waded along the shore, enjoying the fresh sea breeze and the rush of water on their bare feet. Gulls circled and kept an eye out for fish, skimming so close to the water that one good wave might have given them a soaking.

Mara lost herself in her favorite daydream. There she sat in royal white in a palace designed by her father. People fussed over her. Buffing her nails. Fanning her face. Fixing her hair. Arranging her jewels. *Cake for breakfast. Camel races at noon. Dancing beneath the stars with a handsome prince dressed in gold.*

"Hey, dream queen, you're hunching again," said Nathan, giving her his favorite you're-my-weird-sister look. Mara straightened her back. She hated to hunch. She'd never look good on a throne all hunched over.

But after all that had happened, maybe she would look after the horses in the royal stables instead. Or work with leather and fashion the fancy saddles that made an ordinary rider sit proudly. She really didn't want to push people around. Jesus didn't do that, and He was the King of kings!

She could do as her mother did and visit the sick. Or help clean the houses of the old widows. Something, anything, to bring glory to God and make people smile and be glad she was around.

Mara started to hum and Nathan quickly joined in. It was the New Israel club song. Karis looked doubtful.

"Don't worry," said Mara. "You're going to like these words."

> "We are New Israel, kids of strength and might;
> Messiah has loved us, shown us a new light!
> We are strong in His name, brave kids who
>   know what's right.
> We stand the test, 'cause Christ's the best.
> He's given us new sight!"

And in an exaggerated voice, Nathan added, "Greek and Hebrew . . . are . . . all . . . right!"

"Too many lines," said Karis. "Too many syllables."

"Who made you choir director?" Nathan joked.

"Not choir director," Mara said, putting an arm around Karis and looking her way. "You're looking at the club's new vice president."

"Only until the next election," Karis said with a sly smile. "Then I'm running for *your* job!"

"Hey!" Nathan protested. "How come I don't get to be vice president?"

Mara sniffed and held her head high in the queenly way. "You are officially our rabbi-in-training. *Nobody* can do that job like you."

"You really think so?" Nathan asked, tugging his borrowed turban more securely into place. It was two sizes too big. They could barely see his eyes.

"Oh, yes," Mara said, winking at Karis, "I'm absolutely positive."

Letters From Our Readers

Was stoning really a way to execute people in Bible times?

Elisa Barnes, San Antonio, TX

It was a common form of punishment called for in the Law of Moses for crimes deserving death (Leviticus 20:2). An important part of stoning was that all members of the community were to carry out the punishment (Joshua 7:25). Moses and Jesus were both threatened with stoning by angry mobs (Exodus 17:4; John 8:59, 10:31). Saul, who held people's coats while they stoned Stephen to death, himself became a follower of Jesus and was once stoned and left for dead (Acts 14:8-20). He recovered, however, and went on to tell many others about Jesus Christ.

Did people actually eat calf brains?

Brianna Morgan, Springfield, IL

Yes, and not always just poor people. Headcheese—considered by some today to be a delicacy—is made from parts of animal heads, feet, and sometimes hearts and tongues. These parts are cut up fine, boiled, and pressed together into a solid that can be sliced and served. Seconds, anyone?

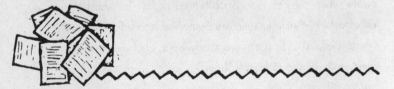

Why did they kill Stephen? Was he doing something wrong?

Carey Reid, Omaha, NE

The Jewish religious rulers didn't believe that Jesus was the Messiah, so when Stephen claimed that He was, they believed he was committing blasphemy against God. (Blasphemy is showing irreverence for God or claiming the attributes of deity.) They also thought Stephen was saying that Jesus came to get rid of the temple and tradition. That really upset them because they were very religious and their traditions were important to them.

Some people believe Stephen was illegally executed because Roman law said that the Jews had no authority to carry out executions without the permission of the Roman government. You can read about Stephen and the Hellenist believers in Acts 6–7.

What were the underground tunnels used for?
Justin Carter, Great Falls, MT

The underground tunnels that Karis and Mara's families escaped through kept the city supplied with water. Jerusalem doesn't get much rain, and it is far away from the Jordan River. Several hundred years before Christ's time, King Hezekiah wanted to be sure that Jerusalem wouldn't run out of water if it was attacked and surrounded by the Assyrians, so he built a tunnel from a place called Gihon Spring (2 Chronicles 32:30). It emptied into the Pool of Siloam. Later, the people of Jerusalem built more tunnels and aqueducts to bring water from the surrounding springs into the city. All of the water had to come from higher elevations because it flowed into the city with the help of gravity.

The tunnels in Caesarea—where Karis was from—
were the city's sewage system. They were built in such a
way that they would be cleaned out by the sea tides.
So, anybody want to go for a swim?

Who were the Hellenists? Why didn't they get along
with the other Jewish believers?

Jessica Lents, Rochester, NY

The word "Hellenism" refers to the Greek culture.
Hellenists were Jews who spoke Greek and followed
Greek customs. Although they were usually from other
places, some were natives of Palestine.

The Hebrews, on the other hand, were Jews who
spoke Aramaic and were from Palestine, although they
were sometimes from other places too. The main
problem between the two groups seems to have been
that the Hebrews followed the Law of Moses and Jewish
cultural practices more strictly than did the Hellenists.
Some of them looked down on the Hellenists, whom
they saw as less righteous or holy. Naturally, that caused
a lot of arguments between the two groups.